This Little Hippo
book belongs to

To Auntie Helen and Auntie Margaret,
two penguins who really are different.

M.O.

To Phillis.

J.N.

Scholastic Children's Books,
Commonwealth House, 1-19 New Oxford Street,
London WC1A 1NU, UK
a division of Scholastic Ltd

London • New York • Toronto • Sydney • Auckland
Mexico City • New Delhi • Hong Kong

First published in the UK in 2000 by Little Hippo,
an imprint of Scholastic Ltd

Text copyright © Maria O'Neill, 2000
Illustrations copyright © Jill Newton, 2000

ISBN 0 439 99627 9

Printed in China

All rights reserved

2 4 6 8 10 9 7 5 3 1

The rights of Maria O'Neill and Jill Newton to be identified as the
author and illustrator of this work have been asserted by them in
accordance with the Copyright, Designs and Patents Act, 1988.

The Penguin
Who Wanted To Be
Different

Maria O'Neill • Jill Newton

Little
Hippo

Dorothy Penguin followed Uncle Binny
up the hill.

"Are we nearly there yet?" asked
Dorothy, puffing hard.

"Almost, Dot!" said Uncle Binny,
taking Dorothy's hand.

They trudged on for a few minutes more
and then scrambled up the last big rock.
They had reached the top of Glacier Hill.

"Look at that view, Dot!" cried
Uncle Binny. "You can see for miles!"
Dorothy gazed down towards the
village. The houses looked tiny.
She could see hundreds of penguins
milling about, some playing, some
shopping, some on their way to the park.

"What do you say to that, Dottie?" asked Uncle Binny, laughing. "Penguins everywhere, as far as the eye can see!"

Dorothy Penguin frowned. "But we all look the same," she said.

The next day, Dorothy wandered into the garden. She was still frowning.

"What's the matter?" asked Dorothy's Mum, looking up.

"Mum, I want to be different," said Dorothy. "I'm just the same as all the other penguins and . . ."

"You are different, Dorothy. You're different and special to me," said Dorothy's Mum. "Now have you written your letter to Father Christmas yet?"

"Not yet, Mum, but . . ." stammered Dorothy.

"Why don't you go and see what
Uncle Binny is doing?" suggested
Dorothy's Mum.
  Dorothy waddled off sadly.
 "Why can't she be like all the other
small penguins?" sighed Dorothy's Mum
as she went back to work.

"Hello Dottie!" said Uncle Binny. "Have you come to help me fix this old sledge?" "Uncle Binny, how can I make myself different?" Dorothy asked him eagerly.

"What a strange question," replied Uncle
Binny, kindly. "Why would you want to
be different when you're lucky enough
to be a penguin?"

"But Uncle Binny . . ." said Dorothy.

"Don't be daft, Dottie!" interrupted Uncle Binny. "Now what are you going to ask Santa to bring you for Christmas?"

"I don't know yet," mumbled Dorothy, kicking up the snow. "I'm going out to play. See you later." Dorothy slid off. She liked skidding on the ice.

Ness and Rory, Dorothy's friends, were playing outside their house.

"Hello, Dot!" giggled Ness.

"Look at our list of presents," said Rory. "We asked for a sledge, two new scarves and a snow wars computer game!"

"And here's our letter to Santa," cried Ness excitedly. "Have you written your letter yet?"

"Not yet," said Dorothy thoughtfully. "But maybe I should."

She borrowed a piece of
paper from the twins and
began to write very carefully.

Here is Dorothy's letter . . .

Dear Santa
  I'm sorry to bother you right now
when you're so busy but I would like
a very special present this year.
  I want to be DIFFERENT!
  That would be the best present
of all. I know you can do it, Santa.
Thanks very much.
                    Love
                    Dorothy xxx
  P.S. I've been very good
  this year. Ask Mum.

Dorothy felt very pleased with herself.
She posted the letter to
Santa and skipped off to play.

On Christmas Eve, Dorothy's Mum
tucked her into bed.

"Goodnight, Dorothy. Sleep well."
"Goodnight, Mum," said Dorothy
happily. "I can't wait until tomorrow."
Dorothy's Mum smiled.

In the middle of the night, an old man with a white bushy beard and sparkling eyes called to his friends.

"It's time everyone," he said. "We have to start work. Hurry!"

A small pixie whispered in his ear.

"What's that?" said Santa. "Two pixies are in bed with flu and one of the reindeer has twisted his ankle. But it's our busiest night of the year," he sighed, "what shall we do?"

Suddenly he remembered a very special letter that he had stuffed into his pocket earlier.

Dorothy was fast asleep and full of
dreaming, when a kindly hand patted
her gently on the shoulder.

"We need your help," said a voice.
"There are so many children to visit and
so many presents to deliver . . ."

"Of course I'll help," beamed Dorothy.
She was so excited she nearly tripped over.
Out of all the penguins in the world, Santa
had chosen her to help.

All night long, Santa and Dorothy and
the pixies and the reindeer flew all over
the world delivering presents.
Until at last they were nearly home.

"This is the last one,
Dorothy," said Santa sleepily.
"Thanks for all your help."

Dorothy carefully put the last present
under the tree and turned towards home.

She quietly climbed back into bed and
was asleep in no time at all. The sleigh
whizzed away into the darkness.

Early on Christmas morning, Uncle Binny arrived. "Happy Christmas! Happy Christmas!" he boomed. "Where's Dottie? Come on, let's go!"

Dorothy and Mum and Uncle Binny
went out to see the big Christmas tree
in the village.

All the small penguins were squeaking
with excitement and unwrapping lots
of presents.

"Look at my brilliant new sledge!"
squealed Ness.

"Look at my new snow goggles!"
shrieked Rory.

There was one very small present
left under the tree.

"This one's for you, Dottie,"
said Uncle Binny. "It's from Santa."
Dorothy read Santa's note.

To Dorothy, a very special penguin.
See you next year! Love, Santa.

She slowly unwrapped the small present.

"Is that all you got?" shouted Ness, zooming past. Dorothy proudly put on her new pixie hat.

"It's just what I wanted," she beamed.

Now, at last, although she looked just the same, Dorothy Penguin felt a little bit different.